A Girl's Guide to Middle School

A Girl's Guide to Middle School

Meredith Shea

Copyright © 2005 by Meredith Shea.
ISBN: Softcover: 1-4134-5847-5
Library of Congress Number: 2004115585

Author photograph © Kathy Singer.

All rights reserved. No part of this book may be reproduced or transmitted in any form or by any means, electronic or mechanical, including photocopying, recording, or by any information storage and retrieval system, without permission in writing from the author.

This book was printed in the United States of America.

This book is for Doctor Helen Holt.
She taught me to have confidence in my work.

Contents

Preface 9

Guys 11
    In General 11
    Just Friends 12
    A Crush 12
    In a Relationship 13
    When Guys Want More 15
    When You Want Out 16
    When a Guy You Don't Like Asks You Out 17

Healing the Heart 21
    No Matter Who Broke It 21
    When It's a Guy Who Broke It 22

Friends 25
    Being a Good Friend 25
    Dealing with Fights 27
    Making New Friends 29

The Internet 31
    Instant Messaging and E-mail 31

Moochers 33

Schoolwork 35
    In Class 35
    Studying 36
    Remedials 38

Your Parents 39
    Limit the Embarrassment 39
    Make Them Understand 41
    Injustice 41
    Family Vacations 42

Siblings 45
    Sister to Sister 45
    Kleptomaniacs 46

Zits and Skin Care 49

Stress 51

Preface

This book started out as a few tips to help my friend, Hannah. After a while, I figured 'If Hannah needs some tips on dealing with this sort of stuff, maybe other people do too.' After I'd written a few chapters for myself and for my friends, I showed my parents. They thought it was great. Then the thought of publishing came to mind. I worked on this book throughout the summer (the summer before I entered 8th grade). After having experienced in middle school most of the situations I have written about, I was surprised at how far I'd come since 5th grade (my first year in middle school). My goal is to help girls entering middle school and prepare them for the ups and downs of it.

Hannah says that my advice helped her. I hope my book helps you. Anyway, middle school will turn out OK. Have fun.

Meredith

Guys

In General . . .

Tip # 1
Remember, girls mature faster than guys. Don't expect too much from them. If you expect anything.

Tip #2
In general, middle school guys are not to be trusted. They pull pranks, lie, act stupid and back stab.

Tip #3
Middle school guys use girls. Be careful.

Tip #4
Never tell secrets to middle school guys. They are motor mouths and spread nasty rumors.

Tip #5
It's tough to avoid all obnoxious guys because they are everywhere. Do your best to keep contact with them to a minimum.

Tip #6
If you must deal with obnoxious guys, deal with them only in well-lit areas, in big crowds, and on a friendly basis.

Just Friends

Tip #7
It's good to know guys who are only friends. It's <u>less stress</u> than a girlfriend/boyfriend relationship.

Tip #8
Being with guys at dances who are just friends makes you never feel lonely. Dance with them and hang out together.

Tip #9
At dances, give guys your screen name and phone number. Keep in touch!

A Crush

Tip #10
Live dangerously. Flirt with him.

Tip #11
Don't send the wrong vibes as if you only want to flirt with him.

Tip #12
Let your friends know you like him. That way they won't go for him or steal the light from you when you're talking to him.

Tip #13
Don't obsess. He's just a boy. Your friends will get tired of you constantly talking about him.

Tip #14
Don't tell his friends. It *always* gets back to him.

Tip #15
Dance. Have fun. Always be yourself. If he likes you then great! If he doesn't then don't worry, there will be others.

In a Relationship

Tip #16
Make sure you're happy with the guy. No one benefits from pity dates.

Tip #17
Make sure your guy doesn't degrade you (put you down) or make you feel lousy. Respect is important in a relationship.

Tip #18
Talk often. You obviously like each other!

Tip #19
Don't talk behind his back. It will most likely get back to him.

Tip #20
Don't jump to conclusions. If you suddenly attack your boyfriend with questions like "Were you with other girls? Where did you go? Why couldn't I reach you?" you're acting more like his mother than his girlfriend. You sound paranoid.

Tip #21
Don't cheat. If you're tempted to cheat on your boyfriend you're probably not happy with him or not ready for commitment. You may want to reconsider your relationship with him.

Tip #22
Be supportive. Go to his sports games. Watch his school play. Encourage him to do the things he loves.

Tip #23
Don't be clingy. He needs time with his friends that doesn't involve you.

Tip #24
Set aside some time to spend with him.

Tip #25
Don't expect too much from him.

Tip #26
Don't sacrifice your friends. They were there first. Guys come and go. Your friends are always there for you.

When Guys Want More

Tip #27
Face it. Most guys will leap at the chance for a more intimate relationship. If you're not interested, just tell him you're not ready.

Tip #28
Leave them if they won't respect you and your decision.

Tip #29
If he threatens to leave you unless you do more, leave him first.

Tip #30
End it. It's not worth being in a relationship with your boyfriend when you think it could end if you don't please him.

Tip #31
Plenty of guys will say they love you and that if you love them you'll do whatever they tell you to do. Don't believe it. Get out of the relationship. They're not worth your time.

Tip #32
Don't give in if you don't think you're ready.

When You Want Out

Tip #33
Don't break up with him in an email. He can forward it to his friends, change the wording, and print it out.

Tip #34
Don't break up with him on instant messenger. He can "copy and paste" everything you say.

Tip #35
Call him, but don't leave a message! If it's his home phone, his parents may end up hearing it first. If it's his cell phone, he can save it and play it for his friends.

Tip #36
On the phone or in person is the best way to break up with a guy. He can't "copy and paste" what you say or show it to his friends. It's his word against yours.

Tip #37
Don't make a scene. If you're with him and a bunch of his friends, you may want to call him later or plan to see him alone another time. You don't want him to hate you for dumping him in front of other people and embarrassing him.

Tip #38
Don't break up with him on a post-it like on "Sex and the City."

Tip #39
Don't ask your friend or his friend to tell him it's over because you're too wimpy to tell him yourself.

Tip #40
Don't lie or make up excuses. Be honest for why you want it to end, even if it makes you sound shallow.

When a Guy You Don't Like Asks You Out

Tip #41
First of all, don't lead guys on if you don't want them to ask you out. If you do, then you'll get a reputation of a tease.

Tip #42
Let him down lightly. Guys take a big risk asking girls out and it hurts to be rejected.

Tip #43
Gently tell him that you would rather just stay friends. You need no other explanation.

Tip #44
After turning him down, change the subject and get on with life. He will get over it.

Tip #45
Don't accept if you're not interested in him and his personality.

Tip #46
Reject him right away. It's better than going out with him, using him, and dumping him and then have him find out later that you never really liked him. Ouch.

Tip #47
If you're unsure about whether or not you like him "like that" just yet, tell him you'd like to get to know him a little better.

Tip #48
Don't go out with a guy to make someone else jealous. It usually backfires and it's not worth your time.

Tip #49
If a guy is persistent and won't take "no" for an answer, don't give in. Tell him firmly that you're not interested.

Tip #50
If the guy continues to bother you, disconnect yourself from him. Sooner or later he'll find a new person to harass.

Tip #51
Never go out with a guy just because you're pressured to. You'll be sorry you did.

Healing the Heart

No Matter Who Broke It

Tip #52
Cry. Let out your feelings.

Tip #53
Take your anger out on your pillow.

Tip #54
Don't hurt yourself. If you turn to cutting and other self abusive things, your scars last forever even though your heart will heal.

Tip #55
Don't mope around and feel sorry for yourself. Exercise and have fun.

Tip #56
Eat some chocolate. They don't call it "Hershey happiness" for nothing.

Tip #57
Write your emotions down. When you're done you'll feel better and you can throw them out.

Tip #58
Get a manicure and a pedicure. You'll feel better and feel beautiful.

Tip #59
Go shopping. Enjoy life!

Tip #60
Give yourself time.

When It's a Guy Who Broke It

Tip #61
Get rid of anything and everything that reminds you of him.

Tip #62
Take your mind off him. Hang out with close friends.

Tip #63
Meet new guys. You'll forget about old what's-his-name.

Tip #64
Enjoy being single. Now you can flirt, dance, and go to movies with lots of different guys.

Tip #65
Take bubble baths. It will relax you and take your mind off him.

Friends

Being a Good Friend

Tip #66
Listen to your friends.

Tip #67
Speak up. Let everyone know your opinion.

Tip #68
Be honest.

Tip #69
Comfort your friends. Give them a hug when they are upset.

Tip # 70
Be there for them when they need you the most.

Tip #71
Give them advice.

Tip #72
Let them know when you're concerned.

Tip #73
Let them know you care.

Tip #74
Compliment your friends. Everyone can use a self esteem boost.

Tip #75
Look out for them.

Tip #76
Stand up for yourself and your friends.

Tip #77
Tell jokes. Everyone loves to laugh.

Tip #78
Talk to them about everything and anything.

Tip #79
Don't be paranoid. Your friends will have other friends, just like you do. That doesn't mean they will just forget about you.

Tip #80
Trust them.

Tip #81
Trust yourself.

Tip #82
Don't be a know-it-all. It will turn people away from you because they feel intimidated by you and inferior. Plus, it's just annoying.

Tip #83
Don't gossip about them. They're your friends.

Tip #84
Stand beside your friends and their decisions.

Tip #85
Share ideas, share thoughts, share dreams.

Tip #86
Be happy for them. Congratulate them.

Dealing with Fights

Tip #87
If a fight is between two of your friends don't take sides.

Tip #88
Be there to talk to.

Tip #89
Spend time with both friends. That way they won't feel like you have abandoned them.

Tip #90
You don't have to be the mediator. They can work it out on their own.

Tip #91
Don't stress over it.

Tip #92
Remember not to get yourself involved too much.

Tip #93
If you are in a fight, allow yourself to relax.

Tip #94
Confront the person you're fighting with after you've had some time apart. Or wait for them to confront you.

Tip #95
Keep in mind, the fight will pass over time.

Tip #96
No matter the outcome of the fight, you will still have other friends who will support you. Give it time.

Making New Friends

Tip #97
Be yourself.

Tip #98
Talk to people. Get to know them.

Tip #99
Be social. Go to dances to meet people.

Tip #100
Throw parties.

Tip #101
Introduce yourself to people at parties.

Tip #102
Meet your friend's friends.

Tip #103
Don't exclude anyone.

Tip #104
Don't neglect your old friends because you've found new ones.

Tip #105
Be outgoing.

The Internet

Instant Messaging and E-mail

Tip #106
Don't say anything you don't want to be "copied and pasted" or forwarded.

Tip #107
Always remember that conversations via E-mail and instant messages can be saved, printed, and distributed.

Tip #108
Don't gossip. It always gets around and can easily be traced back to you.

Tip #109
Don't believe everything you hear. It's easy to frame someone on the internet.

Tip #110
Remember that some people share their passwords so it may not always really be them.

Tip #111
If you need to have a private or heart to heart conversation, have it over the phone.

Moochers

Tip #112
Don't sacrifice anything you need to satisfy another person. A moocher can find another source if you resist the temptation to supply them with their demands.

Tip #113
Don't offer to buy something for someone on a regular basis. That person might grow accustomed to you treating them and ask you to do it more and more often.

Tip #114
When you loan someone money you can't always expect to be paid back. Remind them often that you need your money. That way they won't think it was a gift and come back for more "gifts" from you.

Tip #115
If you don't feel like loaning someone money and they ask for some, you can lie and say you don't have any (not always the best choice), or tell them you need it for something else. Don't give in to anything they say. It's your money. Keep it.

Tip #116
Avoid circumstances involving people who you know use you for your money. If some girls invite you to the movies and you know they mooch off other people, don't be caught paying for their tickets and popcorn. Turn them down nicely and say you have other plans for the money.

Tip #117
Don't leave money hanging out of your pockets. It will attract moochers and you may feel pressured to give it to them.

Tip #118
Generally, it's a good idea to only carry enough money for you.

Schoolwork

In Class

Tip #119
Keep up. If you fall behind it will seem hopeless to catch up.

Tip #120
Ask questions. How are you supposed to learn something if you don't understand it?

Tip #121
Don't cheat. This may seem obvious, but cheating can be an easy way out of studying. The consequences aren't worth it though.

Tip #122
Pay attention. Don't let your mind wander off too far.

Tip #123
Take good notes. It makes it easier to study if you can review your notes when they're well written.

Tip #124
Don't talk to your friends. As tempting as it is, you'll be out of class soon enough.

Tip #125
Don't pass notes. It's not worth getting busted. Plus, on TV, haven't you seen all of the shows where the notes get collected with the homework?

Tip #126
Avoid doodling. As fun as it is, it distracts you.

Studying

Tip #127
Take breaks. It's hard to focus if you stare blankly at something for hours at a time. Get a snack and stretch your legs. It'll help.

Tip #128
Turn off your music. I love to study with my stereo blaring, but I learned the hard way that it's not the way to go.

Tip #129
Chew gum. It can relieve tension. Apparently chewing gum triggers something in the brain that helps with studying. That's a plus too.

Tip #130
Turn off your cell phone.

Tip #131
Don't wait until the last minute. Try to study a few days before. Then you won't be stressed and you'll be better prepared.

Tip #132
Make flashcards. It does help to review them nightly. It takes only a few minutes.

Tip #133
Ask your friends for help. Start a study group.

Tip # 134
Make a practice test. Take all of the information you have been studying and put it into a format that you can do on your own.

Tip #135
Ask your parents to quiz you.

Remedials

Tip #136
Meet with your teachers. You may not be getting enough out of your normal class time. Arrange to meet with a teacher so you can catch up and feel like you're at the same place as the rest of the class.

Tip #137
If you flunk a test, see if you can raise your grade by doing extra credit, doing your test corrections, or retaking the test.

Tip #138
Let your teachers know that you care. If they see that you're willing to work hard and pay attention, you should be able to make some arrangement with them.

Tip #139
Go to the study groups your teachers arrange. Even if you don't have a specific question, you can listen to the other people and learn from their questions.

Your Parents

Limit the Embarrassment

Tip #140
Let your parents know ahead of time some of the things that embarrass you around people. That way, you can prevent them from spilling a mortifying secret about you in a front of people.

Tip #141
Allow them to tell some stories about you. Parents like to show off their offspring because they're proud of you. Let them tell stories that make you look good.

Tip #142
Don't let them dance in front of your friends. Times have changed and they can't dance the way we can. Try as they might they just can't be "cool."

Tip #143
Don't let them bring out the baby pictures of you. Most of the pictures probably involve your bare bottom.

Tip #144
Don't let them sing with the radio. If your parents are good singers, then that's another story. But for the most part, parents lack good singing voices.

Tip #145
When they pick you up and drop you off somewhere tell them not to blast oldies music. Allow them to do so once you are clearly out of sight and nowhere near anyone you know.

Tip #146
When they pick you up, make sure they wear something decent. Tell them not to come in and get you while they're in their fuzzy bathrobe and slippers.

Tip #147
Ask them to wait in the car. Then you can say your goodbyes without your parents breathing down your neck.

Tip #148
Spend time with your parents. That way they won't feel like they have to hang out with you and your friends because they know they'll be able to talk to you later.

Make Them Understand

Tip #149
Remind them that you're not a little girl anymore. You're now in middle school.

Tip #150
Ask for more privileges. Now that you're older, they may consider allowing you to do other things.

Tip #151
Tell them that your friends are like your sisters. You need to have friends, especially in middle school, and you have to make time to hang out with them.

Tip #152
Allow them to ask questions such as "Where are you going? Who are you with? What time will you be back?" It's a parent thing.

Tip #153
Let them know what you want to change. Maybe you want to redecorate your room so it expresses you more or maybe you want to have guys over.

Injustice

Tip #154
Try to reason with your parents, whether it's about your allowance or being grounded.

Tip #155
Don't raise your voice. Chances are you're already in trouble.

Tip #156
See if bargaining is a possibility.

Tip #157
Sweet talk your parents. Don't be too obvious about it though.

Tip #158
Admit defeat. It's not worth losing more.

Tip #159
Tell them you'll be more responsible.

Tip #160
Be helpful.

Tip #161
Earn back their respect, your allowance, or your freedom by being good.

Family Vacations

Tip #162
Spend some time with your family. After all, they did pay for your vacation so you might as well eat meals with them.

Tip #163
Spend time with siblings. It'll mean a lot to them, especially if they're not as outgoing as you are.

Tip #164
Go exploring. Get to know your surroundings.

Tip #165
Meet new people. Talk to the locals and other vacationers.

Tip #166
Don't be shady. Don't randomly and mysteriously disappear. Your family may worry about you and begin to trust you less.

Tip #167
Obey your curfew. Who wants to be grounded on vacation?

Siblings

Sister to Sister

Tip #168
Talk to each other. Update one another on your lives.

Tip #169
Share stuff. Clothes, CD's, games. Save money on things by sharing.

Tip #170
Enjoy each other's company. You're sisters. You're friends.

Tip #171
Listen.

Tip #172
Trust each other. This may not be possible until you are both older and more mature.

Tip #173
Don't tattle on each other. If your sister trusts you not to tell your parents, then you shouldn't betray her.

Tip #174
Spend time together. Cherish every moment you can with each other.

Kleptomaniacs

Tip #175
Sisters share stuff. Sometimes you have to hide things to ensure only you have access to them.

Tip #176
Confront them. Tell them what you're willing to share with them and what is only yours.

Tip #177
If you don't want them to take your stuff, don't take theirs.

Tip #178
If they continue to take your things, have your parents come up with punishments.

Tip #179
If they lose what they borrowed from you with or without permission, make them replace it.

Tip #180
If you let them borrow something make sure you get it back as soon as possible so it doesn't get lost or forgotten.

Tip #181
If you can't find something of yours and you think it's in your sister or sibling's room, ask your parents if you can go in and try to find it when your sibling is away.

Zits and Skin Care

Tip #182
Keep your hands away from your face. The more you touch and rub it, the more oil and dirt clogs your pores causing break outs.

Tip #183
After you exercise and sweat, wash your face.

Tip #184
Keep your pets away from your face. Their fur and the dirt and oil that's in it clogs pores.

Tip #185
Wash your face at least twice a day.

Tip #186
Drink lots of water. Water helps your pores.

Tip #187
Eat healthy foods. Eating a salad can help your skin.

Tip #188
Use a moisturizer on your skin during the day and acne fighting cream at night. Your skin can really dry out from the cream so the moisturizer will give it a break.

Tip #189
Use an oil free sunscreen on your face. It prevents clogged pores and sunburn!

Tip #190
If you get a few break outs on your body, try switching brands of shampoo and conditioner.

Tip #191
Don't wear cover-up everyday. Depending on the kind, it covers zits but also clogs your pores.

Tip #192
Remove any make up before you go to sleep.

Tip #193
If over the counter treatments aren't working, talk to your parents about seeing a dermatologist. Then you can get a prescription that is stronger than the over the counter items.

Stress

Tip #194
Take a break from the situation. Leave it alone for a little while and give yourself a chance to breathe.

Tip #195
Do something you love.

Tip #196
Watch TV. Take your mind off it.

Tip #197
Don't overbook yourself. Make sure on weekends you have free time just to yourself.

Tip #198
Try not to rush around. You'll forget things and it will make everything a lot harder.

Tip #199

Tell your parents what's stressing you out. It may be easier to get rid of than you thought.

Tip #200
Talk to friends. See what they do to eliminate stress from their lives.